The Spick-and-Span Fairy

Published in the United States by
QEB Publishing, Inc.
23062 La Cadena Drive
Laguna Hills, CA 92653
www.qeb-publishing.com

Library of Congress Control Number 2005921180

ISBN 1-59566-066-6

Written by Sally Hewitt
Designed by Caroline Grimshaw
Editor Hannah Ray
Illustrated by Jacqueline East

Series Consultant Anne Faundez
Publisher Steve Evans
Creative Director Louise Morley
Editorial Manager Jean Coppendale

Printed and bound in China

START
Thinking

The Spick-and-Span Fairy

Sally Hewitt

QEB Publishing, Inc.

Every night, Tia and Ben climb into their bunkbeds.

Sometimes Ben wants Tia's top bunk and they have a pillow fight.

4

Every morning, Mom shouts, "You'll be late for school!" so they get dressed and race downstairs.

5

Every day, while Tia and Ben are at school, the Spick-and-Span Fairy makes their beds, folds their clothes, and puts away their toys.

Every afternoon, when they get back from school,
Tia and Ben make their room messy all over again.

Today, Mom has a phone call from Granny.
She looks worried.

"Granny's hurt her leg," Mom says.
"I have to go and look after her."

8

"But who will look after us?" wail Tia and Ben.

"I'll ask Auntie Jo," says Mom.

Tia and Ben love Auntie Jo. She takes them to the park and buys them treats. She has never stayed overnight before.

When Auntie Jo arrives, they all wave goodbye to Mom.

"Send kisses and hugs to Granny," they say.

"Be good!" says Mom.

Tia and Ben play in their bedroom while Auntie Jo cooks supper.

Ben ruins Tia's puzzle, so Tia knocks over Ben's bricks.

Auntie Jo calls, "Supper's ready!" and Tia and Ben race downstairs.

At bedtime, Auntie Jo comes into the bedroom to say goodnight. "What a mess!" she says. "Who's going to clean this up? The Spick-and-Span Fairy?"

Tia and Ben giggle.

In the morning, Tia and
Ben go to school.

When they get home, their
bedroom is still a mess!

"The Spick-and-Span Fairy didn't come today," says Auntie Jo. "You'll have to clean your bedroom yourselves."

The Spick-and-Span Fairy doesn't come the next day, or the day after that!

Tia and Ben have to keep cleaning their bedroom themselves.

17

When Mom comes back from Granny's, Tia and Ben ask, "When is the Spick-and-Span Fairy coming back? We've had to clean our room ourselves!"

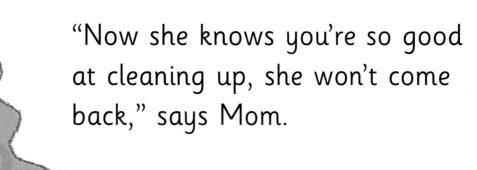

"Now she knows you're so good at cleaning up, she won't come back," says Mom.

"Oh no!" say Tia and Ben.

Mom gives Auntie Jo a big wink!

What do you think?

Why do Tia and Ben have a pillow fight?

What toys do Tia and Ben make a mess with in their bedroom?

Look at page 6. Why is the bedroom clean when Tia and Ben get home?

Why does the phone call make Mom look worried?

21

Look at page 9. Why are Tia and Ben worried?

Why is the bedroom still a mess when Tia and Ben get back from school on page 15?

Is there really a
Spick-and-Span Fairy?

Why does Mom give
Auntie Jo a big wink?

Parents' and teachers' notes

- Look at the cover together and talk about the picture. Can your child describe the cover? What can he or she see?
- Read the title and explain that the title is the name of the story.
- Look through the book, concentrating on the illustrations. Discuss how the story is told by the illustrations, as well as by the words.
- Read the story together, and then discuss what the story is about. Ask your child to re-tell the story to you, in his or her own words.
- Explain to your child that this story is about children of a similar age to him or her. Talk about whether what happens in the story could happen to your child or to his or her friends.
- Talk about how Tia and Ben learn a lesson in the story (i.e., that their mess doesn't get cleaned up by magic, someone has to do it).

- Talk about how Mom learns a lesson in the story, too (i.e., that if she always cleans up after Tia and Ben, then they won't do it for themselves).
- Discuss what Auntie Jo did to get the children to clean up their bedroom. (She told Tia and Ben that the Spick-and-Span Fairy didn't come, so they had to clean up their room themselves.)
- Talk about how magic doesn't really happen in this story. Think of some stories you have read together in which magic does happen.
- Together, make a list of things that your child can do to help at home. Talk about which jobs your child enjoys doing, and which he or she doesn't enjoy.
- Help your child make up a story about himself/herself. Write the story for your child and encourage him or her to draw some illustrations to accompany the text.

I See crrns. I See books

I Se